TALKABOUT

Reflections

TALKABOUT
Reflections

Text: Angela Webb
Photography: Chris Fairclough

Franklin Watts
London/New York/Sydney/Toronto

© 1988 Franklin Watts

First published in Great Britain by

Franklin Watts
12a Golden Square
London W1

First published in the USA by

Franklin Watts Inc
387 Park Avenue South
New York 10016

ISBN: UK edition 0 86313 552 8

ISBN: US edition 0–531–10457–5
Library of Congress
Catalog Card No: 87–50584

Consultant: Henry Pluckrose
Editor: Ruth Thomson
Design: Edward Kinsey
Additional photographs: Zefa
The Zoological Society of London

Typesetting: Keyspools Ltd
Printed in Hong Kong

About this book

This book has been written for young children—in the playgroup, school and at home.

Its aim is to increase children's awareness of the world around them and to promote thought and discussion about topics of scientific interest.

The book draws on examples from a child's own environment. The activities and experiments suggested are simple enough for children to conduct themselves, with only a little help from an adult, using objects and materials which will be familiar to them.

Children will gain most from the book if the book is used together with practical activities. Such experiences will help to consolidate knowledge and also suggest new ideas for further exploration and experimentation.

The themes explored in this book include:

Reflections are light bouncing back.
Reflections can be seen in flat, shiny surfaces.
Reflections are distorted by curved surfaces.
Matt or textured surfaces do not reflect visible images.
Mirror images are pictures in reverse.

Look in a mirror.
What can you see?

Someone who looks
just like you—
the same eyes,
hair and nose?

That's your reflection.

Where else can you see your reflection?

What happens to reflections if water is moving?

Can you see your reflection
in these objects . . .

or these . . .

Exact reflections show
on flat shiny surfaces.

How do they look
when those surfaces are curved?

Experiment with these objects.
What do you notice
about the reflections in each one?

When light falls on smooth shiny surfaces, it bounces back.

Hold a mirror towards the sun.
Can you see the sunlight bounce back?

What else bounces sunlight back?

When you look in a mirror
the whole picture bounces back.
This is the mirror image.

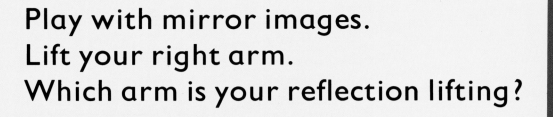

Play with mirror images.
Lift your right arm.
Which arm is your reflection lifting?

Can you shake hands
with your reflection?

Write your name on some paper.
What does it look like reflected?

Can you draw a picture
looking only in the mirror?

See how you can make pictures change.

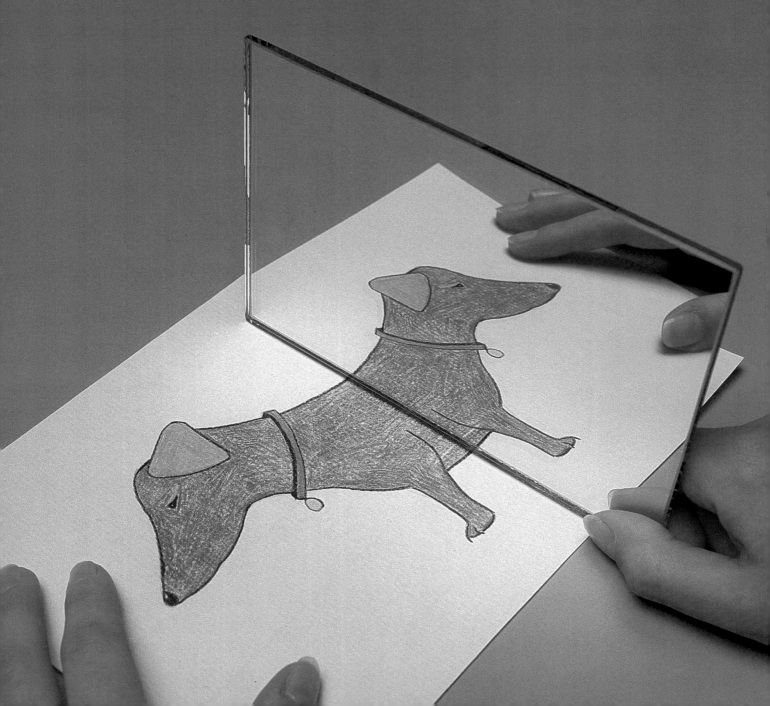

Complete these shapes
with a mirror.

Stand two mirrors together
with something in front.
What patterns can you see?

What happens if you use three?

Can a mirror show you
what's behind you . . .

and inside you?

Look around you.
Reflections
are everywhere. . .

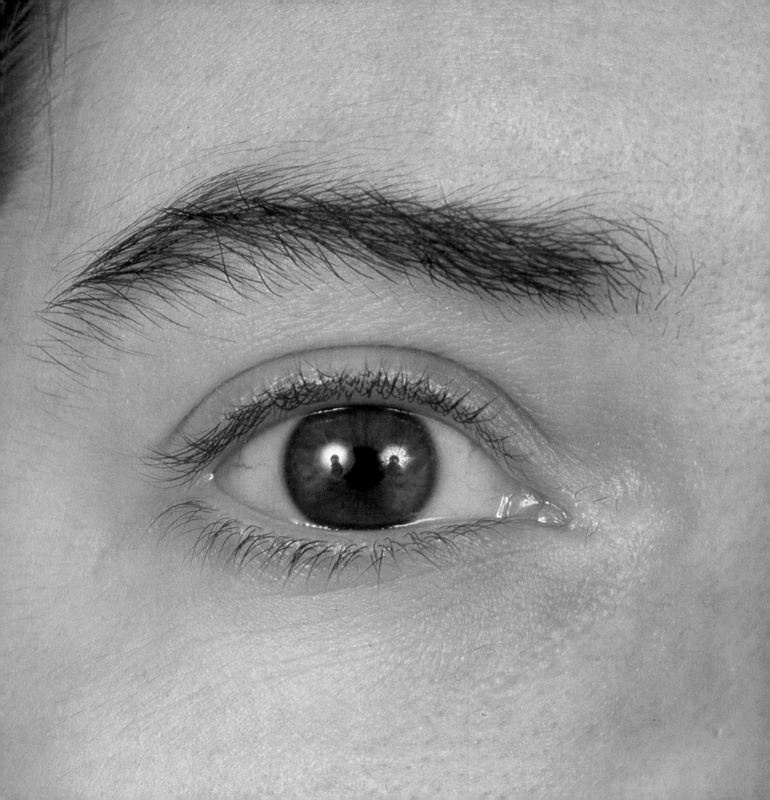

Reflections can be fun.